AF250358

The Curious Kitten

Halloween Madness - Book 4

A Starlight Investigation Short Story

Marnie Atwell

ISBN: 978-0-6450281-6-4

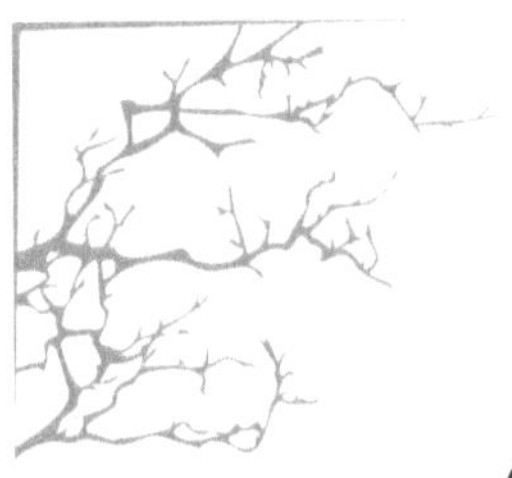

Chapter One

Five hungry kittens raised their noses as they attempted to sort through the scents wafting on the breeze that crossed their forest floor. Their makeshift home provided little protection from the onslaught of smells that assaulted their olfactory nerves.

The rustling from dried leaves produced a shiver of fear in the youngest of the females. Her eldest brother, Champ, raised himself to his full height to provide protection. He allowed her to snuggle closer to him, his body heat helping to soothe her fears. His eyes peered into the distance, seeking the image of his mother.

Champ's attempts were unsuccessful, his eyes having been opened for only one full cycle of the moon. With a few more months behind him, he would be able to see far into the distance. For now, he could barely make out objects more than a metre away.

"Don't worry, Shadow," he said. "Mother will appear at any moment now. You'll see."

She pressed herself deeper into his ginger fur, a striking contrast to the black of hers. Eyes closed tightly against unknown terrors, she whispered, "There is something bad coming. I can smell it."

Champ breathed deeply, acknowledging the smell of bloodied, damp fur. Not having any experiences to call upon, he was unable to give a name to the scent. "Yes, I can smell it, too. But, I can also detect the smell of Mother. She is close."

"Will she get to us before the other smell does?" Ash, the second youngest female with fluffy grey fur, asked. She wandered over to stand beside Champ, creating a more significant barrier for Shadow to hide behind. Mind you, Champ was a roly-poly kitten who constantly glutted himself on his mother's milk making him quite a bit larger than his siblings.

"Her smell is stronger than the other. She will reach us first," Champ assured her. "Where are you going, Stubs? Don't you think you should stay and help me care for our sisters?"

Stubs glanced over at Champ. "I'm pretty sure you've got it under control," he replied matter-of-factly. His blue eyes glistened with intelligence and curiosity as he raked his gaze over his siblings. A slight frown marred his face as he spotted his older sister, Snow, sleeping on a pillow of grass. How anyone could sleep through an entire conversation, let alone ignore the auras of tense emotions was beyond him. Having black fur himself, he kept to the shadows as he made his way towards the oncoming danger.

"I asked you a question," Champ growled, posturing for the benefit of his sisters.

"I don't answer to you," Stubs replied, continuing to move forward without so much as a glance in his brother's direction.

"Go, get yourself killed then. With your stumpy legs and spindly muscles you wouldn't be much help to the females anyway."

Stubs turned to glare at his brother. "The reason you are the best choice to protect our sisters is that you are the most likely to be targeted for food. While our predator is chowing down on you, our sisters will have time to run away and perhaps find a hiding spot before it finishes its meal."

"What a terrible thing to say," Shadow hollered. Ash gazed at Champ and conceded that what Stubs said held a modicum of truth. The predator could kill them all before sitting down to eat. On the off chance it went for Champ first, she would run for her life and worry about the consequences of her actions after, if she were able to make it to safety.

"Where are you going?" Ash asked sweetly.

"To discover what is coming before it arrives," Stubs replied, crouching low as a loud rustling came from a few metres ahead.

Stubs laughed at himself for being so scared. He rose and took a couple of steps forward when his mother leapt into view. She looked frightened, but he could see the determined look on her face as she barely stopped to acknowledge him.

"This way, Stubs," she demanded, not even bothering to turn her head as she reached his siblings.

"What happened, Mother?" he asked.

"Not now, Stubs. Stay here!" she ordered, grabbing the back of Ash's neck with her mouth and carrying her further into the forest. She returned after a few minutes, scooping Champ up by the neck and disappearing from view. When she returned, she looked at Stubs with a very pleased expression. "Thank you for not wandering off," she grinned.

"What happened to your leg? You are running funny, and it smells wrong. What's that stuff on your fur?"

"Later, Stubs," she picked him up and prepared herself to run.

"You should take Shadow. She'll be scared left alone with Snow, who is still asleep."

Mother cat lowered him gently then moved to stand in front of Snow. She noticed the rise and fall of her chest and let out a sigh of relief. Although Snow was a heavy sleeper, the mother cat was astounded that her daughter had managed to remain asleep. She gave her a gentle nudge and jumped when Snow, who had become startled, flexed her claws and squeaked with fright.

"Mother, you scared me!" she cried.

"You need to learn to be more aware of what is going on around you when you rest, Snow. You are putting yourself, and your siblings at risk by sleeping so soundly."

"We are safe here, are we not?"

"No, we are not. We need to go deeper into the forest. Keep your brother company while I take Shadow to safer ground."

Mother cat scooped Shadow off the ground and ran with a more pronounced limp.

"What's going on?" Snow asked Stubs as she washed the sleep from her eyes.

"I don't know," he replied, glancing in the direction his mother had taken. He sniffed the air, surprised the scent of danger no longer assaulted his nasal cavity. His ears twitched as he listened to the sounds of the forest. He wasn't able to detect anything out of the ordinary. "I'm sure Mother will tell us what we need to know when she is ready."

"You should go next," Snow said, licking the fur on her chest.

"No, you go," he returned, crouching into a hunting position as a skink came into view.

"Mother is not going to leave you to last," Snow scoffed. "It would be doubtful that you would still be here when she returned. She seemed tired and hurt. She doesn't need the stress of having to look for you and being separated from us any longer than is necessary."

Stubs bristled at the truth of her words. He wouldn't want to wander off. He was a curious creature that was easily distracted. He pounced for the lizard, disappointed to find it had managed to evade his clutches quite easily. His mother returned and took him by the neck.

"Told you," Snow smirked.

He wanted to keep his eyes open for the journey, but they closed of their own volition. When they arrived at their new destination, he shivered with the drop in temperature. It was dark and gloomy. Gone was the handful of flowers and leaves that were soft beneath his feet. They had been replaced by dust and small pebbles. "Where are we?" he asked.

"A cave," Champ replied.

"What is a cave?" Stubs queried, never having heard the word before.

"This is a cave," Champ answered, surprised that Stubs had even asked.

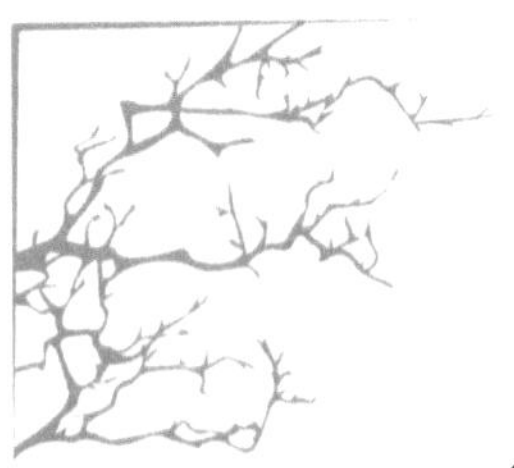

Chapter Two

Stubs growled with frustration, wishing his eyesight was more advanced. He could see the light at the opening but could not determine the distance, nor see any obstacles or pitfalls that lay in between.

Putting on his brave hat, he ventured toward the exit, one paw at a time. He could hear the low mutterings of his siblings but was not interested enough to listen with both ears. The pebbles hurt the pads on his paws. The silence of his surroundings burned his ears. Stubs had barely been there a few minutes before he'd decided to hate his new home.

The light disappeared as an object filled the space. Stubs gasped with fright and crouched down low; a soft growl rumbling in his throat.

"Be calm," his mother's voiced cooed. "It is just me," her voice muffled with Snow's body hanging contentedly from her mouth. He was getting to his feet when his mother stumbled over his body. Snow was flung to the side as his mother fell. He tried to apologise, but his words were lost beneath her thick tortoiseshell fur. The mother cat groaned Snow's name as she tiredly got to her feet.

"I'm okay, Mother," Snow called, also getting to her feet. "It is very dark here."

"Yes, I know. We will be safe here," her mother stated, moving the kittens until they were huddled together. She lay on her side so they could feed.

"Did you bring some mouse or snake?" Ash asked.

"No, love. I did not have time to hunt. I will fetch you something to eat once I have rested. Come, drink some milk, for now."

Stubs moved in to take his share when he felt a paw push his head into the dirt. Even after pointing out the dangers of his gluttonous behaviour to him, Stubs was amused that Champ continued to treat him in this way. He chuckled quietly to himself. What Champ didn't realise was that he was actually doing Stubs a favour. By shortening his meal, Champ ensured Stubs was not so full as to fall into a food coma. It enabled him the chance to investigate his surroundings and practise his hunting skills.

As soon as Champ had filled his tummy, he released Stubs and waddled closer to his mother's face. There he lay down to take a nap while snuggled against her neck. She licked him a couple of times then fell into a troubled sleep. Stubs drank enough to take away the hunger pains plus two more swallows. He stepped back and listened to the sounds of his sibling's sleepy breaths. "Are you awake, Snow?"

"Yes, I'm awake," she replied.

"Do you want to help me explore the cave?"

"No. Let's wait until Mother's awake and she can show us around."

"We could be waiting for ages," Stubs whined.

"Fine, go exploring then, but don't go outside."

Stubs was not going to lie to his sister. Because he wasn't sure he wouldn't end up outside, he chose not to reply. He discovered it was difficult stumbling around in the dark. Especially when the light source was streaming in from above. '*The opening must be up-hill*,' he thought, which seemed to be confirmed by the ache in his leg muscles as he moved.

Reaching a wall of the cave, he took one step after another, ensuring his fur remained brushed alongside the hard, cold surface. By the time he reached the opening, he was panting from the exertion and feeling the beginning pangs of thirst.

Stubs didn't want to disturb his mother further by shuffling down for another drink. Instead, he chose to search for another source of hydration. With a quick glance back into the cave, he placed his paw into the light and felt the thrill of adventure coursing through his veins.

His eyes blinked many times as they adjusted to the brightness. He raised his nose to the wind, performing shallow breaths. The air smelled crisp, but more importantly, free from danger. Stubs took in his surroundings and grinned with wonder. The tall trees provided plenty of shade and protection from the elements. Where there had not been much vegetation at their last place of rest, this area was filled with a variety of plants that had thick green leaves and dainty flowers. Pink, yellow, blue and white coloured the landscape with the sweetest fragrance Stubs had ever had the pleasure of experiencing.

"Oh, Mother," he squealed with delight. "This place is extraordinarily beautiful."

Stubs bounded along the carpet of broadleaf grasses, basking in the dappled sunlight. He frowned as his mind considered his new living arrangements. He had never seen a cave before but was pretty sure he had not just come out of one. It was more like a tunnel, perhaps created by a wombat or a hare. Shaking his head to clear his thoughts, he continued his search for interesting things to look at.

Stubs needed to keep his wits about him or risk the chance of becoming lost. His curious nature had gotten him into some hairy situations which had resulted in him having to be rescued by his mother. He did not mean to be a burden to her and would take extra care while making the journey. His mother didn't smell right, she was limping quite badly. She needed rest. If he didn't find anything in the next half hour or so, he would make the journey back to their new home.

The forest was alive with the sounds of wildlife. Birds were chirping happily in the treetops; while lizards, rats, and mice were scurrying through the underbrush. The temptation to pounce on the moving objects was strong, but Stubs managed to ignore his instincts. He stepped beneath a shrub with soft, purple flowers and froze. He had never seen anything so magnificent in his life. He licked his lips as he crouched down low, his eyes never straying from the vision before him.

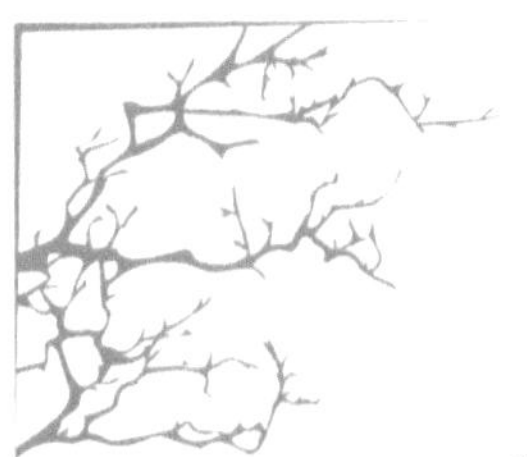

Chapter Three

Scout ventured through the forest, enjoying the solitude of her flight. She breathed in the smell of rotting vegetation and smiled. This was the environment she felt at home in.

There was so much to explore in the forest. She could spend months there and still find new things to delight her senses with. The thing she enjoyed most about this piece of Australia was the preservation of nature. Not a skerrick of litter was to be seen. The people who lived in this community either never went into the forest or took their rubbish with them when they left.

She found many trees that would make the perfect home for a fairy. She gazed around her surroundings, imagining the woodlands filled with them. She felt a pressure in her chest and placed her hand there for comfort. As she fluttered to the nearest branch to rest, she wondered what had come over her.

In the three thousand years she had lived on Earth, not once had she missed her homeland or its occupants. Now she felt herself pining for what was. Her view was limited from where she was perched. While the trunks and branches were long and thin, there were many of them situated closely together. Not happy to be left alone with her thoughts, she leant forward and exhilarated in the fall before her wings spread open and lifted her up.

She moved further into the forest, looking for something to distract her from her musings and the loneliness that ensued. After flying for a few minutes, she found it. With a gasp of pleasure, she fluttered to the ground. "This is amazing," she said aloud with no-one but herself to hear. A small village of fairy-sized mud huts and cobble-stone pathways lay before her. Scout wandered inside the nearest shelter. There was a cluster of round tables that had seating for four. Tablecloths in black material with purple flowers adorned their surfaces. Square plates and round goblets made of clay sat on each table. They were empty and without dust. Somebody had been there recently.

"Hello!" Scout yelled, walking outside. "Is anybody here?" She was met with silence. She could feel eyes on her, but couldn't see who they belonged to. "I won't hurt you!" she cried, hoping to allay their fears. Still, they remained hidden from view. Not a sound to indicate what direction they lay in. It seemed that the huts were all empty. She didn't check them all, but it was quite apparent that whoever lived in this village were currently elsewhere.

'What a wonderful discovery to share with Briella,' she thought. 'Perhaps by the time we get back, the inhabitants will have returned.' Scout had no trouble finding her way back to the pub. "Wait until you see what I found in the forest, Briella," she said as she flew in through the window.

"Scout, you're home," Force said, stating the obvious.

"Hey there, Force. Where are the girls?" she asked excitedly, projecting her thoughts.

"They've returned home."

"Of course," she said, flying towards the door.

"They're not next door. They have returned to the coast," he qualified his earlier statement.

"Oh," Scout uttered as she hovered in place. After she took a few seconds to gather her thoughts, she turned to face him. Being careful to keep an accusatory tone from her voice, she asked, "Why did they leave?"

"April said there was an issue with one of her units that required attention."

"You sound as though you don't believe her," Scout fluttered towards him.

"I don't."

"Why not?"

"I believe she is using her property as an excuse to avoid facing her feelings for me. I would like to pursue a relationship with April, Scout. I think, if she were honest with herself, April would like to pursue a relationship with me, too."

"Force, I need to tell you something." He eyed her body language and sighed.

"What did you do?"

Playing for more time, she said, "What makes you think I *did* something?"

"You are wringing your hands together and biting your lip. Your eyebrows are furrowed, and you are crossing and uncrossing your feet while hovering there in front of me. I suspect out of fear of my reaction."

"Why do you have to know me so well?" she whined, slapping her forehead with her hand.

"Scout, we have worked together long enough for me to recognise a few signals in your body language. I will not hate you, regardless of what you have done. Tell me what it is so that we can move forward," he swiped his hand in the air to indicate she should land on the bench in the kitchenette.

She stood on the hard surface, fumbling with her words. "*I told a lie when you asked about your energy levels.*"

"You said that the excess energy had dissipated."

"Yes, I did. What I didn't tell you was your energy signatures have amalgamated with one another, *Force.*"

He tapped his fingers on the benchtop, "What does that mean?"

"It means that your feelings for one another will deepen. More quickly than they would have had your energies not joined together."

"So I would have fallen in love with her anyway? My feelings for April are not entirely because I used too much power when healing her?"

Scout fluttered up to Force's cheek and rubbed her hand over its surface. "You and April have been in denial for a great many years about your feelings for one another. The healing merely brought your emotions to the surface. You will need to tread carefully. April is so afraid of getting hurt, she would prefer to go her whole life without knowing what it is like to love you than run the risk of losing you."

"She is not going to lose me," he spluttered.

"You can't know that for sure," she answered, thinking about Toren's demise. "You can't promise April you will be there forever. What you can do is promise that you will give her all the love that is inside of you to give. You can promise to love her for as long as you shall live. You can promise that you will protect her with everything you've got." She landed on Force's shoulder to give her wings a rest.

Force smiled, "So, are you giving me your blessing, then?"

"You have my blessing," she smiled and was delighted to find it was genuine.

Force grinned like a man who was standing on top of the world. He leaned back on the stool and steepled his fingers. "So Scout, what are you so excited to share with Briella?"

"Hmmm, I don't know if I should tell you," she narrowed her eyes while contemplating her options. Was this something she wanted to keep just between Briella and herself? She wasn't sure. Scout could tell that Force was going to push the issue, so she figured she would need to come to a decision quickly. He was, after all, her Gatherer and a good friend.

"I suppose I'm out of favour now." Force lifted his eyes to stare at a cupboard attached to the wall as he relaxed his hands on the surface of the bench.

"What is that supposed to mean?" Scout slammed her hands on her hips with a scowl.

"Nothing. Don't worry about it."

"That's a low blow, Force. Guilting me into telling you something that should remain between best friends."

"I thought we were best friends, Scout. I guess Briella holds that position now."

"That is so unfair. I was going to share the most exciting discovery I've made since arriving in this town, but you can forget it. Briella will never take your place in my life. But, if you start carrying on with that sort of nonsense, you are going to find yourself missing out on a lot of opportunities you should be a part of." Scout fluttered into the air and headed for the window.

"Where are you going?"

"OUT!" she projected at him.

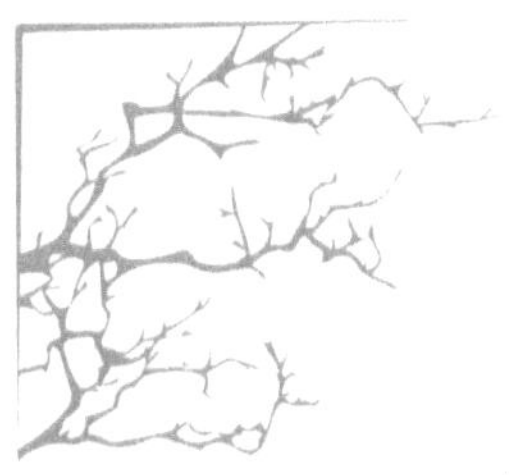

Chapter Four

Scout's cheeks puffed in and out as she tried to control her disappointment. She knew Force had been goading her, but couldn't work out why. Nor could she understand her reaction to his taunts. What was wrong with her?

She made her way back to the village, landing softly on the cobblestones. "Hello," she called with a smile in her voice. "Is anybody home?" Scout sighed deeply as she glanced at the buildings that lay vacant. So many thoughts crossed her mind that she didn't know where to begin. An overwhelming sadness filled her heart. Scout gracefully sank to the ground, placing her elbows on her thighs and her head in her hands. Then she began to cry; mournful sobs that wracked her torso and caused her nose to run.

She was so caught up in emotion that she hadn't sensed his approach. For the first time in a long time, Force had transformed himself into a fairy to follow her into the forest. He hovered close enough to reach his hand out and touch her. Uneasiness at the cause of her sorrow stopped him from taking the final step. His eyebrows furrowed as he gazed upon her. His mouth moved from side to side as he contemplated his actions.

The depth of her unhappiness gutted him. He had never heard anybody cry like that without having been tortured by a monster beforehand. 'What *did that make me?*' he wondered. He wasn't sure what he was going to say, but he couldn't stand to hear her cry a minute longer. He opened his mouth to say her name, but the sound that reached his ears made the hairs on his skin stand on end.

Scout screamed as she peered over her shoulder. Force hovered a few centimetres off the ground, a terrified expression on his face. Behind him, she could see a growling black kitten that was preparing to launch itself at Force. Keeping her voice calm, she sniffled, "It's a young kitten, Force. Don't do anything rash or you might hurt it."

Force's eyes nearly bugged out of his head, "You don't want *me* to hurt *it*?"

"It's just a baby," she managed to get out before Stubs' paws hit his back and he face-planted into the dirt. Scout laughed so hard she got the hiccoughs. While Stubs sat on Force's back with a smug expression on his face, Scout reached into her pocket and pulled out a bunch of tissues. After wiping her eyes and blowing her nose, she said, "Are you all right, Force?"

"Sure, just dandy," he grumbled.

Scout stood carefully, ensuring her movements were slow and smooth. "Hey there, kitty. Come on, off you get." She clicked her fingers, tempting the kitten closer. Stubs tipped his head to the side and mewled. "I won't hurt you," she cooed softly, stepping closer to the kitten. Stubs growled a warning. Scout stopped advancing and began waving her pointer finger at the kitten. "You are behaving like a very naughty pussycat." Stubs rocked on his haunches and launched himself at

Scout, who flew up into the air. Stubs missed his target and pulled off a perfect forward roll. He stumbled to his feet, hissing and spitting.

The second the weight was removed from his back, Force was up and gauging the situation. The kitten was no longer a danger to Scout, she was safely out of reach. From the agitated sounds coming from the kitten, Force realised that not only was he in danger, but the kitten was at risk of hurting itself. There was only one thing to do. Force transformed himself into a kitten of the same size and colour. It took a few minutes to find the connections that would allow him to mind-link with Scout while in cat form. The second they connected, Force began to converse with Stubs.

"Hello, my name is Force," he meowed.

"My mother calls me Stubs," was the reply.

"You seem to be a bit angry, Stubs."

"I am not angry," Stubs assured him. "Just frustrated."

"Why?" Force queried.

"My mother needs me," he said.

"Then why aren't you with her?" Force asked.

"You don't understand," Stubs cried. "She smells funny. Bad."

"Is she injured?"

"I don't know. She is walking funny, and her leg smells bad."

"Where is she?"

"Hiding."

"Show me. I can help," Force nuzzled Stub's cheek with the top of his head. His ears twitched from the sensation of Stub's fur brushing against them.

"No, you will hurt her," Stubs growled.

"No, I won't. I promise. I can heal her."

"How?"

"I just can. You saw me change from a fairy to a cat."

"Can't everybody?"

"No, only a few special people can do this."

"People. My mother said to be wary of people."

"She is right. Some of them are dangerous. I am not one of them. Please, will you let me help her?"

"No," he shook his head from side to side, before running off.

Force considered following, but a quick glance at Scout had him standing his ground. Though she had the slightest smile on her face, her eyes glistened with unshed tears. Stepping closer, he said, "About earlier . . ."

Scout held her hand up to stop him from speaking. "I know what you are going to say, Force. You are sorry and shouldn't have said what you did, blah, blah, blah. Force, you haven't changed. That's the same sort of stuff you have been telling me for centuries. I've changed in the past few days. I'm having a hard time adjusting to always having somebody else around. Then, when I am alone, instead of enjoying it, I find myself beginning to feel lonely, or worse, guilty for loving the solitude."

"Is that why you were crying?" he frowned.

"I was crying because I found this beautiful village . . . you might want to transform into a person my size to see it better." He obliged and Scout held her hand out to him. His grip was gentle but firm. "And when I looked inside, it was clear that the inhabitants of the buildings had vacated them not so long ago. I felt myself longing to meet them, with no idea how long they would be away or if they were even planning on returning.

"I was so excited to think that we would have a community of our own living here that I felt a deep sense of disappointment when I discovered Briella had gone back to the coast with April. I became overwhelmed with sadness when I returned to find the owners of these establishments had not reappeared. I'm afraid I lost it, Force, and burst into tears."

He opened his mouth to tell her it was more than a few tears but was smart enough to keep the thought to himself, in this instance. As they reached the peak of a small rise, Force felt excitement bubble up inside him. At that moment, he felt like a little boy exploring a mysterious jungle.

He ran towards the buildings, pulling Scout forward. She yanked her hand out of his, moments before losing her balance completely. Her wings fluttered furiously, preventing her from a nasty fall. "Well, I never," she muttered, reaching up with her right hand to brush her fringe to the side. She viewed his child-like antics with a smile on her face.

'Aw, how cute.'

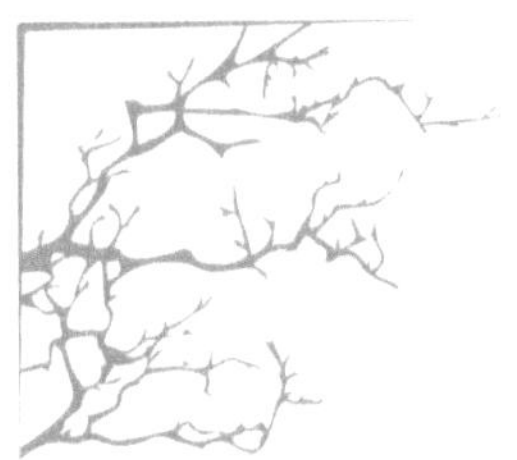

Chapter Five

Stubs ran home. He alternated between glances over his shoulder and keeping an eye on the path. It took him twice as long to return. He was gasping for breath and thirstier than ever upon arrival.

In his fright, he didn't notice the small scratches that covered his face from diving through bushes to hide his short stature from view. He was terrified that his little venture out would lead to the discovery of his family's location by the male and female in the woods.

Who knew what they would do to his loved ones. His mother had warned him on many occasions of the dangers in going out on his own. She had also used many words to provide him with a horrifying picture of the humans that stole little kittens from their mothers so that they were never seen again.

While she told her stories, he pictured creatures much larger than the two he had left behind. She hadn't mentioned the fact they could take on the forms of other animals. Perhaps, that was what made them so dangerous. Maybe, she had only ever seen them in giant form.

Either way, there was no telling what she would say or do to him if he were to articulate what he had been up to. Hopefully, she would still be sleeping when he entered the cave, or tunnel as he had come to think of his new home. Stubs crept over to the opening and stuck his head inside. The darkness had wrapped its arms around his family, making them invisible to his eyes.

He took a deep breath and thought brave thoughts before taking a few steps inside. Stubs stood still for a few minutes, allowing his eyes to adjust. The first thing he noticed was a slight movement in his peripheral vision. His body began to shake. He could have let fear take over, but he was smart enough to know that if anything dangerous had been in there, his mother would have taken care of it, sick or not.

"Hello, who's there?" he said, puffing out his chest and protracting his claws.

"Where have you been?" Ash's voice cut through the darkness.

"Checking out our surroundings. I thought I might be able to find mother something to eat," Stubs answered steadily.

"Why?"

"She is not well and needs some help. We can't rely on her forever to satisfy our needs. It is probably for the best if we start to learn how to take care of ourselves, don't you think?"

"A mother takes care of her kittens, Stubs. It is the natural order of things. Why can't you just be happy with the way things are? Why do you want to change things all the time?"

"Survival of the fittest, Ash. Those that are willing to take risks and try new things will have a greater chance of survival."

"Or a shorter lifespan and an earlier grave."

"What are you two arguing about?" their mother asked.

"Sorry to wake you, Mother," Stubs said, rubbing his head against her chest. "Did you have a good sleep?"

"Yes, fine. Come away from the entrance," she said, grabbing Stubs by the neck and expecting Ash to follow. She carried him to the others and placed him gently on the ground. "Look after each other while I get us something to eat. Stay here, all of you."

"We will," the kittens chorused.

"Stubs?" she questioned.

"I said it too," he whined.

"Promise?" she said, needing some extra assurance before leaving him behind. She knew he had been out but was too tired to search for him. Luckily this time, he had come home safely without the need for any intervention from her.

"Yes, I promise," he said, swallowing his irritation to appease his mother.

"I won't be long."

Once they could no longer hear the padding of their mother's paws, Snow wriggled herself over the top of her siblings until she was sitting beside

Stubs. She didn't want the others to hear, so she whispered in his ear, "What did you see out there?"

"It's very pretty outside, Snow. There are dainty flowers in exquisite colours, and oh, the perfume; It's simply divine."

"What else?" she asked, her eyes growing more prominent as images began filling her head.

"The trees are taller, and the leaves are a darker colour. The shrubs are not as dense, therefore, easier to huddle inside to hide."

"Ooh, it sounds lovely," she squealed a little louder than she meant to.

"What are you two going on about?" Champ grumbled.

"Nothing you would want to talk about."

"Who says?" Champ growled.

"Nobody," Stubs said, hoping Champ would let the conversation die a natural end. The 'harrumph' Stubs received as a reply told him his strategy was right on the ball where his brother was concerned. He waited a few seconds before continuing, "You are going to love being out there, Snow. I guess you will have to wait until Mother says you can go outside before you see it, though. You being such a good girl and all."

"I don't always do what I'm told. I only stayed behind to keep an eye on Shadow. She was feeling a bit scared after the move, and I didn't want her waking Mother. We both know how that would have ended."

Stubs did know. They would have been in a lot of trouble, and he would have been given an extra scolding for leading Snow astray. "Next time Mother goes to sleep, I'll show you what it's like out there, as long as you promise we won't be gone long. Champ, I'm sure, would have no qualms about waking Mother to tell her you are missing."

"Yeah, you could be right about that."

"What are you going on about, Stubs?" Champ snarled, moving closer to the duo.

"I was asking where the best position is to have a nap. I'm a bit tired."

"Well, the best position does not belong to you. We all get first pick of the softest, most comfortable place to sleep before you."

Stubs sighed before nipping the tip of Snow's tail which she used to lead him to a snug corner in the back of the tunnel. He lay down and closed his eyes. "Do you mind if I stay with you while you sleep, Stubs, even though I'm not tired?"

"Of course not," he mumbled before sitting up in a hurry. He narrowed his eyes as he said, "Unless you are planning on doing something while my eyes are closed?"

"No, I wouldn't do that. Lie down. You'll be safe with me."

He fell asleep within seconds of his head hitting the dirt.

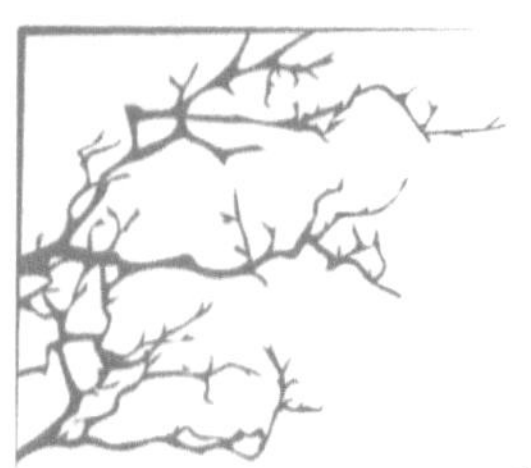

Chapter Six

Force spent the rest of the afternoon exploring the village and its surrounds with Scout. He had hoped Stubs would make another appearance. He would like to be given another chance to convince the poor little thing to let him help his mother. Force worried that the mother might die without assistance leaving Stubs, who was too young to fend for himself, to perish also. Force had already decided to take Stubs home with him if he refused to give up the location of his mother. Until he spotted him again, there was nothing more Force could do.

"I suppose we should head back," Force said, noticing the darkness creeping in.

"You go," Scout replied. "I'm going to stay out here tonight."

"For what purpose?"

"You know I like to sleep in the forest. I don't like being enclosed in human buildings."

"Then why didn't you say something before April began building you a house?"

"I don't know. She seemed to find happiness in creating it for Briella and me. I didn't want to disappoint her. I will only need to sleep in it when Briella and April come to visit. Besides, Briella will need somewhere to stay when she comes. She doesn't like sleeping in the forest.

"She lives in her house within April's home at the coast, but that is not natural. Briella needs to start acting like a fairy. The Purge is coming. She will need to be prepared for its arrival, and she can't do that while living in April's pocket, so to speak."

"What does The Purge have to do with anything?"

"We will be relocated to Fairyland prior to the commencement of The Purge. Briella will become an outcast if she continues to act like a human. She will be in unfamiliar territory because there will be no way for her to get back to Earth."

Force looked aghast. "Perhaps she should stay here then. We could hide her."

"That won't be necessary. Dynopiah, the wood nymph we met a few days ago, said that we had at least a decade to prepare. Briella will be ready by then."

"What makes you say that? The Starlight Investigation team are not going to let the two of you live together full-time. You both have areas of Australia that are your responsibility to keep safe. Where do you think Briella is going to live when she is not here?"

"In her house at April's place," Scout sighed.

"Don't worry about it now, Scout. We've got plenty of time to devise a rescue plan for Briella. Do you think the fairy that was assigned to this area before you built this village?"

"No," Scout shook her head. "While these are lovely, they are not our style of dwelling."

"Who do you think could have created them?"

"Probably some of the local children. They probably bought them at the shops and then set up a play area where they could let their imaginations run wild."

"But the furnishings are free from dust. That means somebody has been here recently."

"Jacinta spends a lot of time in the woods, Force. Now that she has become friends with Calamity, she has lots of children to play with. Perhaps it is another group of kids. We might never know. We can't very well stay here until their return. It could be days, or even months before they come back to play."

"You're right," he said. His thoughts went back to the kitten. "Have you spent much time in this part of the forest?"

"No, that was the first time I've ventured here," Scout admitted. "Have you?"

"No. There must be a water source nearby for the mother cat to be raising her kittens there. Would you mind helping me find it, Scout?"

"Not at all. Why does it matter?"

"If she is injured, she may not be able to hunt effectively."

"So, if you can find the water source, we can leave some food there for them to eat," Scout finished for him.

"Exactly," he grinned broadly.

"What kind of food are you thinking?"

"Well, I was hoping you would continue surveying the area while I ducked to the shop to pick up some dry food."

"Sure, good idea. That way, the food won't go off before she can find it."

"Stay safe," he said as his body grew to its usual size. Without a backward glance, he headed towards the pub to retrieve his bike and his wallet.

It took her half an hour to find the small creek that meandered through the woods. She shook her head at herself. '*Girl you are always heading off in the wrong direction when you don't have a monster's signal to follow,*' she thought. She landed carefully, mindful of disturbing any paw prints that might be visible along the bank. Strolling with downturned eyes, she searched for any sign of a feline's presence. A few minutes before Force's return, she found them. Allowing the mind-link to take place, she guided him to her location.

"*This would be the perfect place to leave the food, Force. See the paw prints in the dirt?*"

He placed the container of food he'd brought with him on the ground before shrinking himself for a better view. "I agree," he stated with interest. He pointed to a spot over her shoulder, "Why don't we wait over there by those trees?"

"As long as it's downwind, it should be a great spot to lay in wait," she stated.

But the mother cat never came.

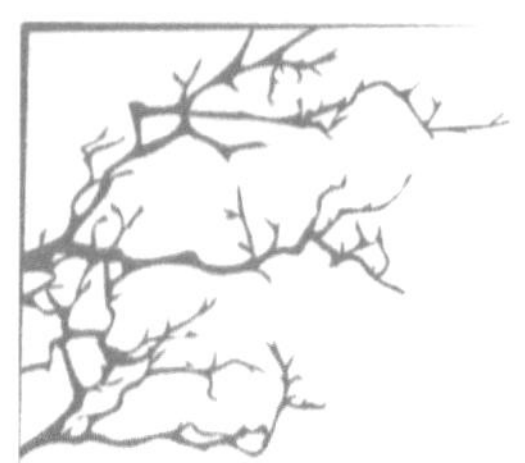

Chapter Seven

Stubs was getting itchy feet. It had been two days since he'd had the opportunity to leave the tunnel. His mother had ventured out for little bursts, always returning before he and Snow could make their preparations to go. Stubs worried that his mother wasn't eating and said as much. She simply smiled in return.

Having been inside the tunnel for so long, his eyes had adjusted to the darkness. He figured there had to be a light source coming from somewhere further along the hollow because he was able to tell the difference between night and day without having to move closer to the entrance. Not being given another chance to exit through the opening, he convinced his sister to explore their new home further.

"Where are you two going?" their mother queried.

"We are checking out our new home, Mother. That's okay, isn't it?" Stubs replied.

"Don't go too far," she warned, not having had a chance to explore their new home herself before relocating her family.

"We won't," Snow said excitedly.

"Can I come?" Ash asked.

"Of course," Snow replied before checking with Stubs.

He simply stared at her. She bowed her head, knowing she had displeased him.

"Does anyone else wish to come?" he asked. When he didn't receive a reply, he looked to his sisters and said, "Come along then."

After half an hour of walking, they realised they were indeed in a very long tunnel. The further they travelled, the darker it became. There were a couple of places that had small holes in the ceiling that allowed light to filter through. Once they moved past those places, though, it took a while for their eyes to readjust to the gloom, wasting precious minutes.

"This is boring," Ash grumbled.

"Turn around," Stubs commanded with a deep sigh. He had known she would start complaining sooner or later when he'd allowed her to come. "We'll head back for a drink. I'm getting thirsty anyway."

Feeling deflated, Stubs trudged back to his mother with his sisters. He was going to go out of his brain if he had to stay in the dark for an hour longer.

"Did you have a nice time?" their mother asked.

"No," Ash growled. "It was boring."

"Is that right?" mother cat asked, spotting the scowl that Snow gave Ash. "Snow?"

"It was nice to be able to stretch my legs for a bit," she answered.

"I suppose you are all feeling the same way," mother cat said.

"I'm not!" Shadow cried. "I like it here."

"You like it here because you are hidden away, Shadow. You need to learn to embrace life. You can't hide in the darkness your entire life."

"Why not, Mother?"

"You need to learn to hunt and fend for yourself. I won't be around forever."

"You'll be around long enough to take care of me until I'm old," Shadow pouted.

"Get up, all of you. We are going on a grand adventure," their mother stated.

Stubs was so excited he almost bumped into her on his way to reach the exit. Mother cat leaned forward and gripped the back of his neck between her teeth. Lifting him up, she grinned when squeals of outrage poured from him. Slowly, she limped towards the opening, giving her young a chance to keep up. She ignored Stubs outburst knowing the position of her hold and the rocking motion of her movement would lull him into submission.

Mother cat led them over the damp terrain that would take another day or so to dry out after the downpour of the previous night. The raindrops glistened on the blades of grass, the leaves of the trees and the petals of the wildflowers that grew in abundance along the water's edge.

The kittens gasped with awe as their eyes took in the beauty of their surroundings. They breathed in the crispness of the air and enjoyed the cool morning breeze as it ruffled their fur. Everything that moved in the wind became prey to be stalked or hunted. She led them to a bend in the creek that had a safe platform for them to learn from. Placing Stubs at her feet, she said, "It is time for you to learn how to drink water."

"What is water?" Ash questioned.

"Why? I like your milk," Shadow sulked.

Mother cat showed them where to put their feet so they wouldn't lose their balance and fall into the creek. Next, she showed them how to use their tongue to scoop up the water. The kittens tried this new technique with varying amounts of success, beginning with Champ and finishing with Shadow. "I am so proud of you my little kittens," she said quietly, focussing her attention to the other side of the bank. Scout knew she had caught the attention of the mother cat when the feline herded the kittens together and crouched into a predatory pose.

Mother cat licked her lips as the creature landed on the petals of a daisy flower. She glanced from right to left, looking for a way to cross the river without getting wet. To her annoyance, there weren't any low hanging branches to climb, or dead tree stumps with which to cross the quickly flowing stream of water. She determined she would need to get her feet wet if she wanted to secure a tasty meal for her kittens.

"Stay where you are," she warned her kittens as she began to stalk her prey. The movements of her front legs were slow and precise. As for her back leg, well, the pain that came from being in that position was almost enough to make her abandon the idea.

"What is mother doing?" Snow whispered.

"Hunting," Stubs answered softly. He was too interested in watching his mother hunt so he could learn how to do it, to tell his mother that he knew the creature.

Mother cat's hesitation was short-lived. The pride in Stub's voice encouraged her to resume a stealthy approach. She stepped into the stream, bracing herself against the cold and the pull of the water. The creature seemed to be unaware she was being hunted. The mother cat reached the middle of the creek, careful to place her paws amongst the pebbles.

The fire in her leg was almost unbearable, but she continued to move forward. The opportunity to show her babies how to catch their food was too great to pass up. Her leg was getting worse with each passing hour. She needed to do something to ensure her kittens survived should her injury get the better of her. Almost to the edge of the bank, she heard a sound she hadn't wanted to hear, the fluttering of wings.

"NO," she yelled as she watched the creature fly away.

A glance over her shoulder told her why. Three little kittens were bouncing excitedly on their paws. Stubs was perfectly still, learning with watchful eyes. Snow was asleep at his side.

Mother cat extended her claws and swiped at the bank in anger. A growl ripped through the air as she unleashed her frustration. After gaining control of her emotions, she limped back to her kittens and led the way home.

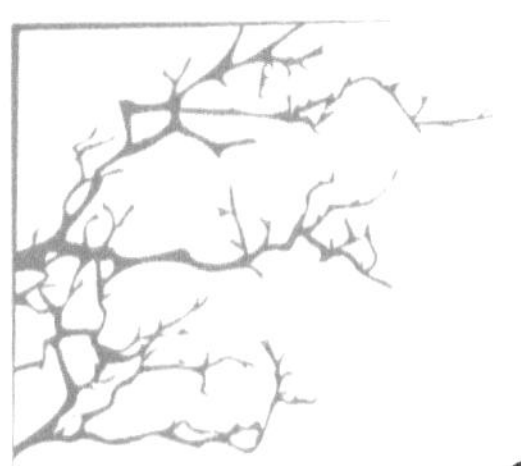

Chapter Eight

Scout watched them leave from a safe distance, determined to find the location of their home. Although aware the mother cat hunted her, Scout knew she would have had a relatively good chance of being captured had the feline not been injured. Once she discovered their hideaway, Scout hurried home to notify Force.

She flew through the window, "I know where they are!"

"Who?" Briella asked, thrilled to see her friend.

"Briella," she cried, fluttering to her friend and hugging her firmly. "It's so good to see you. Where's Force?"

Briella raised an eyebrow, "Good to see you, too. He's next door, saying hello to April." Scout took off for the door. "What's got you in such a hurry?"

"There is an injured cat with kittens that needs help," Scout threw over her shoulder. "Wait until you see what I discovered in the forest."

"What is it?" Briella asked, chasing after her friend.

"I'll show you later," she said, "It's too impressive to ruin with words. I can assure you it will be worth the wait. How did it go back home?"

"Great," Briella said.

"You seem to be more at ease with yourself," Scout observed.

Briella shrugged, "Nothing went awry while I was away. Halloween is getting closer, and my magic has behaved itself over the past couple of days. Perhaps, the danger is over."

Scout felt a little disappointed to think that the drawings Briella had completed may not have a way to come to life to give the people in their new community a thrill on All Hallow's Eve. She did feel relieved, however, that Briella was no longer feeling fearful of what might happen if her emotions were to become excited.

THE CURIOUS KITTEN

The fairies flew into an uncomfortable situation that was developing between Force and April. She appeared to be experiencing discomfort at having him stand too close to her personal bubble. He seemed to be annoyed that she was trying to distance herself from him. Scout entered the room and said, *"I've found them, Force. Come quickly."*

He spun around on his heels and asked, "Who?"

"The cats," she said, annoyed that he had forgotten them so quickly. When she glanced at April, she could hardly blame him. He definitely had his work cut out for him.

"Lead the way," he said, instantly transforming into fairy form. April and Briella remained rooted to the spot, surprised expressions on their faces as Scout and Force exited the room swiftly.

April glanced at Briella, "Any ideas?"

"Scout said something about an injured cat."

April frowned, "Why would that make him leave in such a hurry?"

"Apparently, she's got kittens."

April quickly composed herself and hurried out the room.

"Where are you going?" Briella yelled.

"To give them a hand," April answered. She found them quickly and followed on foot. Stepping inside the forest, she contemplated turning herself into a fairy as well but decided one of them should stay in human form. Their healing abilities didn't work while they took the appearance of another being. She wasn't as agile as Scout and Force who could zip around obstacles quickly, sometimes flying right through the middle.

She tried to keep her footsteps light, and to avoid stepping on anything that would make a lot of noise. The last thing April wanted to do was alert the cat of their presence and have her runaway without receiving the medical attention she required. Scout landed on a branch and pointed to the burrow. "They are in there."

Force glanced down and nodded. He flew to the entrance and contemplated walking inside, but thought better of it. Force felt Scout behind him before he saw her. "What do you think?" he asked her.

"I think we should send you in there in your cat form. If you look like a kitten, the mother might be less inclined to hurt you. Then you can ascertain the situation and report back with information that could make the retrieval go a lot smoother."

"Won't she be able to smell that I am different?"

"Probably. She will be more defensive than normal too. Either way, you will probably get scratched up, if not bitten," Scout grimaced.

"Nah, I'll be right. The mother cat will be able to sense my intent. She will know that I am not there to hurt her or her kittens."

"If you say so," Scout said.

Force morphed himself and entered the burrow cautiously. He wanted to appear as though he was lost and in need of help. The mother cat sensed his presence and growled menacingly. He froze on the spot, afraid of what she might do. Her next move was quite surprising. She deferred to Stubs, who quickly moved between his mother and the newcomer. "Don't hurt him," Stubs cried.

"You know this kitten?"

"Yes," Stubs answered.

"From where?"

"Out there," he answered.

"Please, can you help me? I seem to have become lost and can't find my way home."

The mother cat stepped forward, her kittens looking on curiously. She sniffed Force oddly, her nostrils curling up at the bottoms. "You smell of human," she growled, grabbing Stubs by the leg and dragging him behind her.

"I live with them," Force acknowledged. "They have been good to my mother and me."

"Then how is it that you became lost?" she probed suspiciously.

"I like to explore my surroundings," he glanced towards Stubs. "and got carried away."

The mother cat accepted his explanation without question. She had a kitten afflicted by the same traits as the newcomer. She was not well enough, however, to take on the responsibility of another kitten. With regret, she said, "I am sorry young one. I am not in a position to help you."

Force was stunned by her reply. She must be feeling worse than he had realised. "Could you at least take me to the edge of the woods? I am sure that once I am out in the open, I will be able to find the farmhouse I came from."

"You live in a farmhouse?" Ash asked, taking a step forward. "What is that?"

"A big house that is cool in summer and warm in winter," Force replied.

"That sounds wonderful," she sighed.

"What do you do for food?" Stubs asked.

"The humans give me food to eat, plus whatever my mother catches when she hunts."

"You are fed by your mother and the humans?" Champ asked.

The mother cat was unsurprised by his response. She knew she was not feeding him what he needed with her leg the way it was. She wondered if she should allow her kittens to be raised by the humans who were looking after the newcomer. His fur shone with health as did his eyes. Would she be doing the right thing by trying to care for her kittens when there might be a better option?

"Would your humans be willing to take care of my kittens?"

"Sure," Force replied. "But why would you not want to take care of them yourself?"

"I am injured. I cannot care for them any longer."

"What are you saying, Mother?" Ash asked.

The mother cat ignored her, staring at Force while she waited for an answer.

"My humans would take care of you too if you would like to live with them."

The mother cat looked at him sadly, "I don't think so."

"You are going to abandon us, Mother," Stubs growled. His eyes glowed with animosity.

"I love you all immensely. I want you to grow up to be healthy, happy felines. You will not have that opportunity if you stay here with me. You will all die of starvation," she told them truthfully, no longer able to hide the seriousness of her injury. "This kitten can provide you with an opportunity to flourish."

"A loving mother would stay with her kittens," Stubs grumbled with an accusatory tone.

"I will see you safe," she promised. "Come, kittens, let us see if we can find this young one's home."

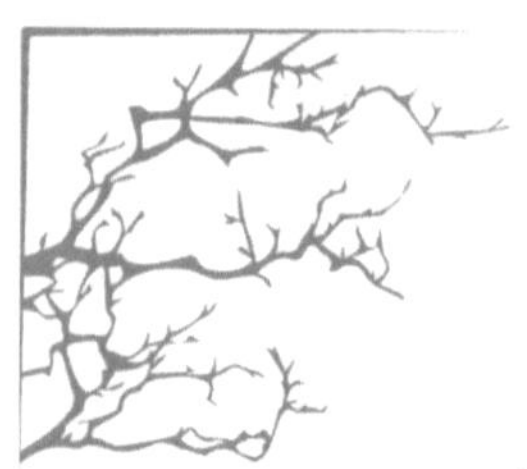

Chapter Nine

Force snuggled into the mother cat's coat. He rubbed his head beneath her chin and tickled the fur on her chest. "Let me check to ensure it is safe out there for your kittens. Wait until I return before making your way outside."

"That is not necessary, little one."

"I insist," he said, making his way towards the opening.

Stubs lurched out of his mother's reach, "I'll come with you."

Once they were close, Force said, "My friends are waiting outside to help your mother. Do you think she will be upset when she sees them?"

"Maybe," he muttered. "Is she going to die?"

"No, we are going to heal her. There are too many of you for my friend to carry on her own. I will need to turn back into my human form to get you all back home. You will have to go in there and encourage her to come out first. Tell her that I have decided to stay out here as a lookout."

"Okay," Stubs agreed, making his way back inside.

Force established a link with April and quickly apprised her of the situation. She was ready to act when the mother made her appearance. The moment her head poked out of the hole, April fussed over the kitten in her hand. "Who is your friend, Smoogie?" She leant down and placed Force at the foot of a native ginger plant. She then turned her attention to the mother cat. Remaining in a kneeling position, she called to it tenderly, "Hey there, kitty. I won't hurt you." She clicked her fingers quietly, "Come here, and let me take a look at you."

The mother cat meowed softly, "Is she safe?"

"Yes," Force mewled back.

The mother cat crept forward, the pain in her leg evident. She stayed just out of reach of April as she studied her intently. April held the back of her hand out to the cat, making sure to remain a few centimetres away. The cat sniffed her, recognising the scent from the newcomer. 'This must be the kitten's human,' she surmised.

"Your leg doesn't look too good, does it? I'd like to have a closer look if it's all right with you?"

Force moved forward and rubbed himself over her leg. April chuckled quietly, "Yes, I know. You don't like my attention being on anyone other than you." She picked him up and returned him gently to the base of the ginger plant. "Stay there, Smoogie."

By this time, the mother cat had moved within reach. April reached out slowly and ran her fingers over the cat's back. "Now, let's have a look at that leg." April grabbed the cat beneath the tummy and lifted her off the ground, tucking her firmly against her body. Then she ran her hand over the leg and scanned the flesh, bone, muscle and tendons for the source of the problem. She was horrified to discover the cat had a serious gunshot wound and that the injury had since become infected.

April murmured softly to the cat as she extracted the bullet and sent healing energy into the wound. The cat struggled slightly as her leg began to heat but soon settled down again once the pain started to lessen. After a few minutes, the leg was good as new. April rubbed the cat's cheek and got a nip on her thenar eminence (the part of the palm below the thumb) for her troubles.

"Ouch," she howled, giving her hand a couple of shakes. "Naughty kitty."

She put the mother cat on the ground and viewed her irritably. She glanced at Force, "Nice friend, you have there, Smoogie."

Stubs meowed bravely as he raced to stand by his mother, protecting her. The mother cat gave an answering meow, warning him off. Humans were definitely not creatures you'd want to be tangling with. Force padded towards the mother cat, "Will you let my human take care of you and your kittens?'

"No," she stated decisively. "My leg is healed, and I am quite capable of taking care of my kittens."

"Until next time," he cautioned. "You know, if you were to live with my human, you and your kittens would have a safe place to roam, hunt, and rest peacefully."

"What makes you so sure?"

"My humans are highly respected in the human world. People wouldn't dare come onto their property to shoot their animals. My humans would likely shoot back, and get away with it."

"Is that the truth?" she asked.

"Yes."

"Fine. We'll give it a trial for a few days, see how it goes."

"Great," Force replied. "I'll let my human know."

The cat looked at him funny. Force decided it was time to let her in on his secret. She thought he was joking until he transformed himself. She became spooked and ran back down below. Stubs ran in after her.

"You lied to me, Stubs."

"No, I didn't, Mother."

"You told me that kitten was safe."

"He is."

"He is a human," she hissed, furious at him for placing them in danger, "who knows where we are."

"The lady fixed your leg, Mother. They are good people."

"That is beside the point."

"You said you would look after us. We would have died if she had not healed your leg. I think we should give them a chance."

"He is dangerous, Stubs."

"Why?"

"Because," she struggled to find the words to explain her feelings. "He is not right."

"He is special. Like the woman. Imagine what our life would be like with them in it."

She did. They could bring them danger just as easily as protect them from it. She looked at their faces. She could tell, they had believed the human's words and wanted to live somewhere like that.

"A few days," she cautioned.

"Thank you, Mother," Stubs grinned. He hurried outside to see if the humans were still there. Force and April were where he left them. He meowed at them excitedly. It took Force a couple of seconds to make the connection with Stubs while in human form. "I missed that little buddy. Say again?"

He was surprised when Stubs complied. Force passed the information onto April, suggesting they carry one kitten in each hand. That meant the mother would have to walk along beside them, which wouldn't be a problem now that her leg was better. Provided, of course, she had the energy to make it that distance. She hadn't been eating sufficiently. Force figured they should make a quick stop for some dry food and a drink of water before beginning the trek home to the pub.

He waited for Stubs to send the cats out before they made their way to the creek. The mother cat was grateful for their hospitality and would have overeaten had it not been for Force's cautionary words. The walk home was uneventful, but they ran into a bit of trouble when they arrived at the pub.

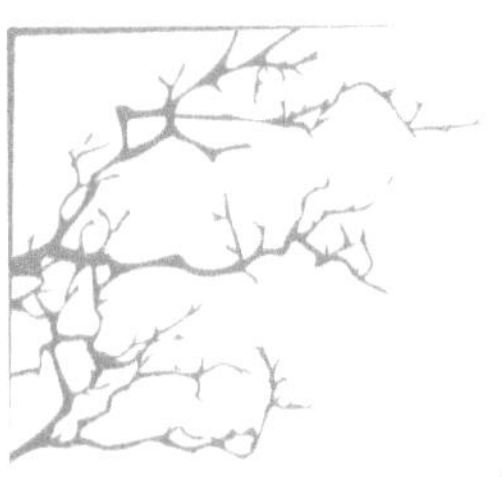

Chapter Ten

Force and April used the back entrance to avoid bringing any attention to themselves. Unfortunately, Robbie had taken that moment to dash to the toilet before the next lot of patrons started making their appearance. He hopped from one foot to the other, as he said, "You can't bring them in here."

April blinked her eyes in surprise at the gruffness of his voice. "They are tiny kittens in need of a home. Their mother has been injured and needs a few days to recover."

"That may be the case," his face softened slightly, "but I'm running a business here, and they are not allowed."

"Nobody will even know they are here once we have hidden them behind closed doors," she said.

Robbie was going to wet himself if she kept him any longer. "I'd love to oblige your wishes, April . . ."

"Then do it," she butted in. "We'll be gone soon, and they will have loads of room to run around in at our new place. They are too little to leave out there with no supervision."

He peered at the cat weaving her way between their legs. "They have a mother," he replied.

"What if she gets shot again? She might die this time."

"She looks okay to me," he jiggled on the spot.

"Well, she's not," April's voice roughened slightly. "I wouldn't argue with you if I wasn't concerned about their safety. I will make sure they don't make a mess and will clean it up if they do. Please, Robbie. Just a couple of days?"

"Fine," he said, running for the bathroom. "You remember this when you are being railroaded by a suspect."

"Where do you think I learnt it from?" her raised voice followed him through the door. He chuffed slightly before letting loose with a curse. She grimaced guiltily hoping she hadn't caused him to have an accident. They hurried up the staircase and fought over which room the cats would be situated in. April won the argument. Force hoped his decision to concede would gain him favour at a later date.

Briella was excited to see them return until she spotted what they held in their arms. "What are those things doing here?"

"We are going to take care of them," Scout answered happily. "Aren't they cute?"

"Sure, for now. They will eat you when they get bigger," Briella warned.

"No, they won't. They will be our friends, protecting us from other predators."

"You think?" Briella viewed them distastefully. "I'll be staying with you until they leave."

"They are coming with us to our new home, Briella."

"I see," she fluttered to the window and stared outside. The mother cat jumped up beside her and startled her. She too, peered out not giving Briella the slightest bit of attention.

"I don't think you have any worries about your safety," Scout stated.

"Sure, while everybody is looking. Wait until she gets hungry and wants to feed her kittens."

"There will be plenty of food for them to eat," Scout assured her.

April collected her handbag from the countertop. "You girls be right here while I grab some kitty litter and a tray?"

"Hardly," Briella said sourly. "I'm going next door."

"Do you want me to give them to Force to look after?"

Briella studied her face. "No," she admitted, noticing the stress lines had disappeared from her forehead. "They'll be fine here."

"I won't be long," April promised.

Force wanted to go with her but thought it best to keep an eye on the fairies. He was awarded a grateful smile from April. Determined to get away from the kittens, Briella suggested Scout show her the surprise she had been saving for later. Scout's face became highly animated as she pictured the images she was about to share. *"You'll be right here, Force?"*

"Of course. The cats and I will get to know each other while you are gone."

He grabbed a couple of shallow bowls from the cupboard and filled one with water and the other with dry food. He sent April a text requesting a few tins of different flavoured wet food for the kittens to try. He worried that their milk teeth were not strong enough to withstand the biscuits. The mother would not be able to hunt for them until settlement of their new home took place.

Force watched the fairies leave through the window with a touch of jealousy. He wanted to walk through the village and observe Briella's response to seeing it for the first time. A small black kitten flopped its body against his foot, sending the feeling of missing out far away. He scooped the kitten from the floor and carried it to the centre of the room where the coffee table was. He sat down and soon had kittens trying to climb all over him. The mother cat sat at the window, peering into the distance.

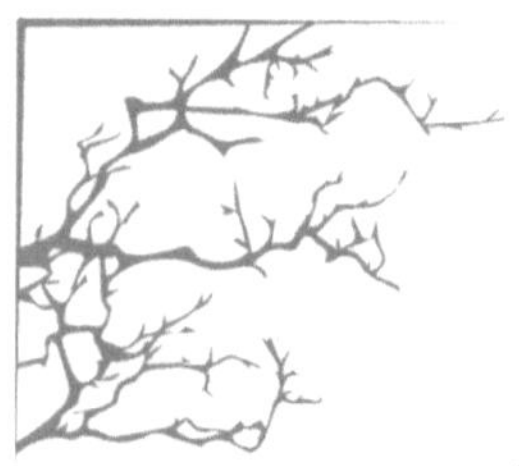

Chapter Eleven

Briella had a spring in her step as she wandered through the village. She assumed the persona of a voyeur as she perused the quaint cottages with their cobblestoned borders. Various expressions adorned her face as she absorbed every sight, sound and smell. Her heels clicked loudly on the hardened surfaces, squelching unpleasantly when she went off course.

She peered inside a building, leaning casually against the doorframe. Her arms were crossed over her chest, and her legs were crossed elegantly at the ankles. "Hmmm," she murmured as her eyes raked over the furnishings. "The occupants have style."

"It's nice, isn't it?"

"It's all right." Briella stepped further into the building, her eyes never staying still. "There are no doors or windows, only openings."

"Our houses back home were like this, open and airy."

"Small and unsecure," Briella contradicted.

Scout held her tongue. She wasn't about to get involved in an argument. She could tell that Briella was more excited than disappointed by her discovery. That was good enough for her. "Do you think these belong to fairies or humans?"

Briella whipped her head around swiftly. "These were not put here by one of us."

Scout was disappointed by the conviction in her tone. Even though she had come to the same conclusion herself, there had still been some hope in her heart that fairies other than the Locator Fairies shared the Earth with them. Scout found the loneliness creep in. She gave herself a mental shake, hoping her outward appearance remained unchanged. "How is our house coming along?"

Briella's face brightened. "It is finished. April just needs to put it together at the new property. I thought I let you know that before we left for the coast. Sorry."

Scout waved her apology aside. "Let me show you the garden before we leave." Scout escorted her outside and took her down the wavering path. In the middle of the village was a small plot of soil with the most gorgeous bunches of dahlias growing in the dappled sunlight.

Briella gasped with delight as she lowered herself to sit among their leaves. She ran her fingers over the petals, which were soft and smooth. "How beautiful," she breathed softly.

Scout grinned broadly, "I thought you'd like them. Want to take a couple home?"

Briella gave her a quizzical stare. "You don't think they will hinder our flight home? They are a bit big."

Scout studied the flowers critically. "I believe you are right," she determined. "We should come back tomorrow with the jeep."

"Great idea," Briella laughed happily. An ominous growl had them jumping with fright. That, combined with the thought of going for another ride in the remote-controlled car, had the production of fairy dust kicking into overdrive within Briella's body. It burst from her pores like an exploding powderpuff.

Luckily, Scout was outside of the firing line. Unfortunately, Stubs was not.

He had been looking for his family when he heard the fairies talking. The yearning for his mother temporarily forgotten as curiosity took hold. He tried to fight the compulsion to seek out the source of the noise, for that was what got him separated from his family in the first place. He had heard a rustle in the bushes and curiosity had gotten the best of him. By the time his curiosity had been satisfied, his whole family had disappeared. But once again, he was unsuccessful. The emotion was too powerful.

He had snuck up behind the fairies, hoping to pounce on at least one of them, if not both. Their wings fluttered slowly, the anticipation of their capture increasing exponentially. He lowered his front legs and wriggled the stump of his tail, preparing to launch, let out an ominous growl akin to "Geronimo" when the assault of Briella's fairy dust occurred.

He sneezed explosively, the dust irritating his eyes enormously. He rubbed them with tender paws. He could hear the shocked voices of the creatures but wasn't able to see them. His eyes hurt too much to open them. He cried, wishing his mother were there. He felt tiny hands rubbing the fur on his chest and fluid pouring over his eyelids. Soon, he was able to pick out the shape of their bodies from the grass. A few more minutes enabled him to see a fuzzy version of their faces. Fifteen minutes later, he was able to make out their features entirely. He blinked a few times, but not because his eyes were still hurting. He could have sworn the fairies were taller before the dust cloud smothered him.

"Oh my goodness, Scout. Look at what I've done!" Briella shrieked with dismay as his body transformed before her eyes.

Scout's incredulous gaze swept over the changes in his physiology. "It's okay, Briella. Don't panic."

"Don't panic? It looks like we left a kitten behind, and now I've turned him into a monster. What if there are more of them out here?"

"He is not a monster and you didn't leave him behind, I did. As for leaving more behind, I doubt it.

They would be together, don't you think? I bet this is Stubs. He was the one Force and I met first. He seems to be a very curious kitten who tends to wander off. I bet that's how he got left behind."

Briella shook her head, totally ignoring Scout's explanation. All she could do was fixate on the effects of her troublesome magic. "Of course he is a monster, Scout! Just look at him. He is the size of his mother. Look at his colouring. Where did those grey and white stripes come from? Where has his shiny black fur gone? What if he doesn't change back? He looks like a white tiger cub, but with a thinner head."

"Briella, you've got to stop panicking. Your magical mishaps always right themselves by dawn. Why don't we get him to follow us home and let Force and April deal with him."

"His mother is there. She won't recognise him. She will think he is a threat to her babies and might hurt him."

"Well, what do you suggest?"

"I don't know what to do," Briella cried unhappily.

Scout gave her a cuddle, keeping a watchful eye on Stubs. She wondered if they were in more danger now that he was the size of an adult. She hoped he still had the outlook of a young kitten, playful but not too serious. Scout had to admit he could kill them both with a single swipe of his paw if he got too carried away.

Stubs sat down and swished his tail. He peered at it with surprise. Gone was the stub that had given him his name. In its place was a long, normal-looking tail, albeit the wrong colour. He mewled with happiness that he had a fully functioning tail, then noticed that the fur on his leg had also changed shades. His heart grew heavy with despair that his glossy black fur had been replaced with white and dark grey stripes.

He tried to communicate with the fairies, but they couldn't understand him. Stubs knew that they were somehow responsible for the transformation in his appearance. He wanted to know where his mother was and felt the fairies might be able to help find her. He worried that she would not recognise him if he did manage to find her.

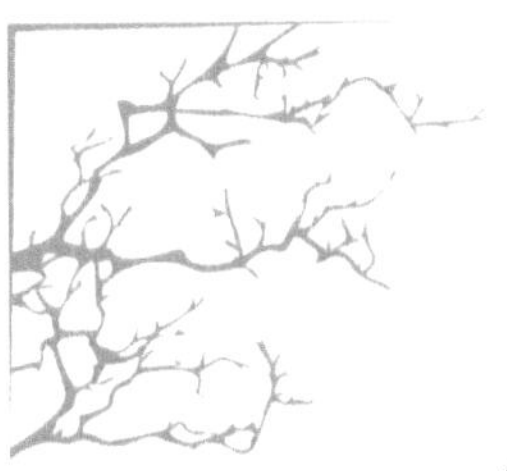

Chapter Twelve

Briella paced in a tight circle, being careful to keep her wings as still as possible. She couldn't stay motionless to think, and she didn't want to give him an incentive to attack. Underneath his new façade, he was a baby who had not learnt to take care of himself properly.

His mother had not had the opportunity to teach him to hunt effectively for his food. He was also unskilled in defending himself against another tomcat or predatory animal. Briella was desperate to work out a way to keep him safe until he reverted to his usual self and could be reunited with his mother.

Briella turned to Scout, "He is going to die, isn't he?'

"Why would you say that?"

"He can't take care of himself."

"We can take care of him," Scout said calmly.

"How? I can't use my magic without things going wrong."

"We won't need magic to look after him. There is dry food at the creek. We left it there for his mother, but he is big enough now to eat it himself. Actually, it is probably just as well he is the size that he is. Otherwise, he would go hungry."

Briella scowled at her, "If he wasn't this big we could have reunited him with his mother. She could have fed him and protected him."

"One of us would have gone to the pub and waited for April's return if she was still out shopping before Force could come back to collect Stubs. That would have left one of us alone with him. A baby but, potentially, a dangerous, predatory animal. I think it worked out better this way. We can take care of him until the morning if we have to. April or Force will come looking for us when we don't return."

"Do you have your phone on you?"

"No," Scout replied. "I tend to leave it at home these days with Force remaining in the area."

"We could send a distress signal."

"This hardly constitutes a situation that warrants an action as drastic as that. We will be fine, Briella. You are worrying too much. Let's see if we can get him to follow us to the creek."

Scout and Briella walked backwards so they could keep an eye on Stubs. He watched them with keen eyes, lowering his front legs into a killer's crouch. Briella turned her head in Scout's direction but was too frightened to take her eyes off him. She whispered out the corner of her mouth, "Do we fly?"

"Not yet," Scout murmured back. "We are too close. He will capture us before we have lift-off."

"When?"

"I'll let you know," Scout answered, hoping she would get the timing right.

His irises flickered in size as his eagerness grew. The capture of a fairy would be a considerable boost to his confidence. He had watched his mother keenly when she had taken them to the river. While his siblings had not been able to contain their excitement, he had sat quietly and observed the way she had manoeuvred her body while hunting her prey.

Had he not growled behind them, he would not have been covered in fairy dust and would have had one of them in his grasp already. A mistake he would not make again. He could not come at the fairies the same way his mother had. As far as he knew, Scout had been unaware of his mother's presence. The creatures in front of him were fully aware he wanted to catch them. How to accomplish that was something he was not sure how to do.

His opportunity came when Briella's heel got caught in a piece of grass. She lost her balance and was falling when he took a swipe. He scooped her up in his paw and grinned as he brought her closer to his face. She panicked and screamed at the top of her lungs, the sound hurting his ears immensely. He shook his head swiftly from side to side and let her go. She landed with a thump in a cloud of dust. Getting to her feet, she brushed her clothes down with a scowl. Scout held her belly with her arms as she cried with laughter.

Briella stamped a foot, "Stop it, Scout!"

"That was the funniest thing I've seen in ages," she giggled.

"I don't think it is funny at all," Briella stormed.

"Of course not," Scout hiccoughed. "It happened to you."

"At least he didn't eat me."

"Thank goodness for small mercies," Scout agreed still chuckling.

"Will you stop it?"

"I can't. I wish I had captured that on video. You would be laughing too."

"Highly doubtful," Briella sniffed. "Let's get back to the job at hand, getting this guy some food. It will be dark soon."

"Sure. How about we try to confuse him. You fly left, and I'll head right. Hopefully, he won't know which of us to go for first. By then, we will be too far away."

"Sounds good," Briella said. "On three?"

Scout nodded and counted. They flew up into the air, and as expected, he hesitated long enough for them to get a reasonable distance away before coming together again. Scout hovered in the air, encouraging him to track them. Then, she fluttered away, thrilled to see him weaving around bushes and leaping over fallen branches to keep them in sight. When they reached the spot where the dry food was located, Scout found a low-lying branch to land on.

She pointed to the forest floor, hoping he would understand her desire to look for the biscuits that were scattered there. Stubs looked at her uncomprehendingly, but then his nose sniffed the air curiously. He searched the area expectantly before detecting the path to the delectable scent. In his excitement, Stubs pushed his nose into the dirt before pulling back slightly. He had found one of the biscuits and scooped it up with his tongue.

He crunched on it satisfyingly before seeking out another. After a few minutes, he found he was thirsty and headed towards the creek. He stood how his mother had taught him and after a few failed attempts, managed to drink his fill of water. A flurry of wings brought his head up with a snap. A pigeon had landed not more than a few metres away. Stubs licked his lips and lowered his body to the ground. "Hmmm," he meowed softly.

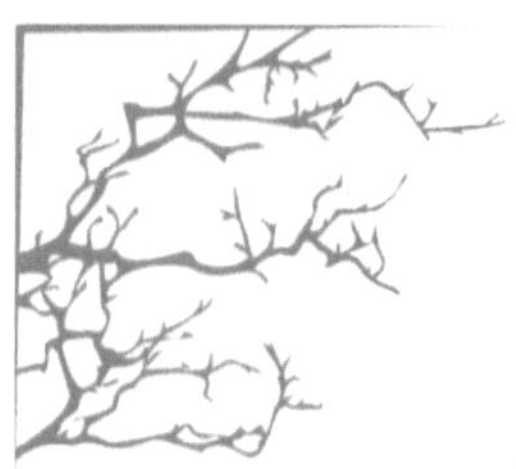

Chapter Thirteen

The fairies covered their faces with their hands. They knew what Stubs hoped to achieve and that what he attempted was a natural instinct in felines. They just didn't want to watch the outcome of his actions. Should he be successful in his attempt to capture the bird, he would surely kill it and begin to consume its carcass. If he failed, they didn't want to see the disappointment that would surely be plastered across his face.

Briella tapped Scout on the arm, "If he kills the bird and eats it, do you think we could go back home for the night?"

Scout narrowed her eyes, "Leave him out here on his own, *all night*?"

Briella twiddled her fingers. "It was just a question."

"You were terrified for his welfare before. What has changed?"

"Nothing," she shrugged, trying to appear blasé. "I just thought if he could take care of himself . . ."

"And what happens when the sun comes up, and he transforms back into a kitten, or a fox comes trotting by and decides he would make a great meal."

"We could be back before dawn and the chances of a fox trotting by is . . . "

"Highly likely," Scout interrupted. "I've seen one hanging around for the past couple of nights. It is probably the reason the kittens' mother got shot in the first place. It is most likely hungry and looking for an easy meal. What could be easier than him?"

Briella settled herself on the branch, her legs swinging gently beneath her. "You are right. We should watch over him and make sure he is okay."

"You managed the night out here when the scarecrow came to life," Scout reminded her.

"That was different. He was like a ninja warrior."

"From what I heard, he was copying your moves, Briella."

"The cat won't do that. He won't be able to protect us if we get into trouble."

"We won't need protecting. Besides, once the cat has finished with the pigeon, we will head back to the village. It will offer us protection from any night creatures that might come across us. We will be able to keep an eye on the cat while he sleeps. In the morning, you can go and get Force, because April will be busy with the mother cat and kittens."

"Sound good to me," she cringed as they listened to him kill his prey. "I think I am going to be sick."

"Why don't you go and find us some food to eat?"

"What?" Briella retched. "How can you think of food at a time like this?"

"It will be dark soon, Briella and we won't be able to see very well to fly. It can get quite dark in here at night with the canopy of the trees above us."

"Fine," she stated. "It beats staying here listening to that."

Briella flew away and collected some mushrooms, placing them on a table inside one of the cottages. She chose a building near a plot of dirt large enough to allow the cat to stretch out if it wished to. Then she gathered a selection of wild berries to keep them hydrated throughout the night. Figuring she couldn't delay her return any longer, she made her way back to the branch to find Scout waiting patiently for Stubs to finish his dinner.

Briella felt like she was returning to a crime scene. Feathers were scattered everywhere, some with bits of flesh still attached to the calamus. She wondered if she would ever feel like eating again. Briella did marvel at the swiftness with which Stubs devoured his meal and the fact that he hadn't wasted any of the bird. She wondered if the head had been eaten before quickly pushing that thought away. She really didn't want to know. "How're things?" she asked instead.

"Fine," Scout said. "He should be ready for a nap now that he has eaten. We should probably make our way back to the huts."

"Great idea. How are we going to get him to follow?"

"I don't know. He is not likely to chase us after that huge feed."

"If he doesn't come with us, you should sprinkle him with dust and levitate him there," Briella suggested.

"That will work," Scout said with a nod. She wasn't going to leave him there alone for the night, but she didn't want to remain out in the open herself. Stubs couldn't understand their words but decided to follow them anyway. He had a belly full of food and was feeling quite content, though he did not want to be left alone. He seemed to work out the gist of their pointing and figured they wanted him to settle on the blanket of dirt for the night. He puffed up his fur to keep himself warm and curled himself into a ball. He closed his eyes and was dreaming of running with his siblings in no time.

Scout and Briella sat at the table and shared one of the mushrooms. Scout chose to finish her meal with a slice of strawberry while Briella elected to munch on a blackberry. Then they chatted throughout the night about a variety of subjects. The thought foremost on their minds was the relationship between April and Force and how that would impact their lives.

"I don't understand what her problem is," Briella lamented. "She likes him, he likes her . . ."

"Look at what happened to Toren. How would she cope if something happened to Force?"

"Would it hurt any less, just because she decided not to date him?"

"Maybe," Scout shrugged. "I've never liked anyone enough to want to date them."

"Liar," Briella laughed. "If you could have made yourself permanently big, or Force could have made himself permanently small, you would have had a crack at it."

"True," Scout grinned. "I imagine it would hurt more to lose someone you were dating than someone you were good friends with. Having said that, you can't live your life in fear that your loved one will die. Think of all the happy, special moments you would miss if you lived like that. We have got to do something to convince April to give them a chance. Imagine how happy she will be when they begin living their lives as a couple."

'Yeah, imagine," Briella whispered, a conniving grin on her face.

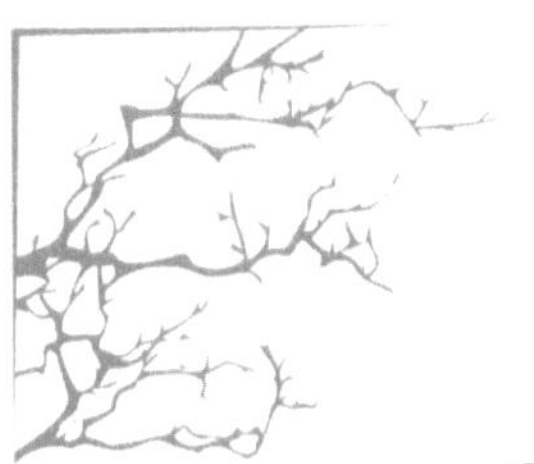

Chapter Fourteen

Snarling from outside had the fairies jumping to their feet. They dashed outside to see a large tabby arching its back and hissing at their kitten. Briella raised both hands to her mouth while Scout couldn't manage anything other than a face-palm. They viewed the scene with horrified eyes unsure of how to proceed.

"Do something!" Briella shrieked.

"Like what?" Scout shouted. Now that she was faced with a daunting situation, all ideas flew out of her head.

"I don't know." Briella yelled. "If I get any magic on them, who knows what will happen."

"They will most likely become the size of a panther," Scout answered helpfully. "What if I put the other cat to sleep?"

"Then what, you levitate him somewhere else?"

"I could," Scout nodded slowly, seeing the holes in her plan. The cat would eventually wake and return to finish what it started. "We can't let the kitten fight the cat. He will get hurt."

Briella looked around for something that could help them. "How about we grab one of those branches lying over there and chase the cat away?"

"Do you think we would be able to lift it? It looks a bit heavy."

"You could magic it, and make it lighter. We only really need the end bit with the leaves. It should be enough to scare the cat away."

Scout flew to the branch with the most foliage. She sprinkled a bit of dust and with Briella's help, lifted it off the ground. They fluttered to a spot above the two cats then swished the end between them. The tabby ran a few metres before stopping. He spun around and glared at the fairies. Stubs ran in the opposite direction. He got as far as the other cat before completing the same actions. The cats eyeballed one another. Scout and Briella gripped their weapon more tightly. "Seriously?"

The fairies flew after the tabby cat, screaming a battle cry at the top of their lungs. They held their weapon in front of them, the tip wavering wildly as they struggled to maintain its weight. The tabby took off in fright. Even though he left the safety of the forest to run across the open meadow, they continued to follow. Stubs chased after him. "Don't," Briella yelled out to him, but he didn't listen. Stubs was running, and he was enjoying the chase. He hadn't thought about what would happen if the cat stopped and faced up to him. He only wanted to play.

Stubs growled. He didn't mean to issue a challenge. It was an involuntary action. The cat spun around and arched its back, yowling menacingly. Stubs screeched to a stop, hissing instinctively. The cat rushed forward and took a swipe at him, cutting the bridge of his nose. Stubs howled in pain, upset the cat was behaving so viciously towards him. The cat wanted him out of its territory, but he had nowhere else to go. All Stubs wanted to do was to play and to find someone to help him locate his mother. The cat did not know that Stubs was just a kitten. How could he? The cat treated Stubs the same as he would any other cat and took another swipe.

Stubs cried again, striking out in self-defence. He managed to catch the tabby on the tip of his ear, bringing a scream of outrage to the fore. The cat retaliated swiftly, pouncing on top of Stubs. He bit him on the side and kicked him with his back legs. Stubs screamed with pain. Briella shouted at Scout, who flew over the top of the fighting felines fully prepared to sprinkle her dust.

The cry of another cat caught the tabby cat's attention. He lifted his head and listened keenly. In the blink of an eye, the cat tore himself away from Stubs and bounded in a southerly direction. Stubs grumbled to his feet, licking his fur with long, tender strokes. The fairies looked at him sadly. Briella said, "I wish we had brought a lantern with us. Then we would be able to discern his injuries. Do you think they are serious?"

"I don't think so," Scout shook her head, "but he might get an infection if we don't take care of it soon. Cat bites can cause a nasty abscess. "

"Can it wait until morning?"

Scout shrugged. The extent of her interest in the local fauna, extended to which creatures posed a danger to herself and which she could ignore completely. "We can try to coax him to the pub so that April and Force can look him over."

"You don't sound confident at all," Briella scowled. "We can't leave him here, bleeding."

"The pub is too far away for us to be able to keep his attention. We could lose him before reaching the halfway mark. If only the cat had taken off in the pub's direction."

"Yeah, that would have been helpful. Don't worry, Briella, he'll be fine. Cats fight all the time. It can't be too big a deal, or there wouldn't be as many of them around."

"They have huge numbers in their litters, Scout. Perhaps, that is because most of them don't make it to adulthood."

"Fine. How do you want to do this?"

"I don't know. I was hoping you would have a good idea."

A cat meowed in the distance. Stubs stopped bathing himself and listened. The fairies dropped their weapon and Scout flew in front of his face and hovered. "Don't you even think about it," she scolded. He swatted a paw at her. She just managed to raise herself in time. "Oh, you are a naughty boy." He gave her a calculated look but became distracted by the cats caterwauling in the distance. He took off at a fast pace with the fairies in hot pursuit. "Obviously, his injuries are not too severe."

"Hmmm," Briella responded. "Maybe you should have hit him with your magic after all."

"Indeed," Scout said, slightly out of breath.

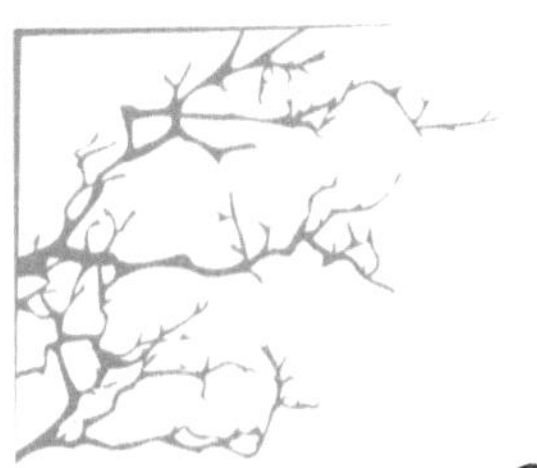

Chapter Fifteen

They came upon the tabby who was circling a grey female with ginger patches. She had a slim face and a sleek body. She was hissing at him plenty while he returned growls in low tones. Scout and Briella searched for anything they could use as a distraction. Stubs was about to get himself into a world full of trouble. He puffed out his chest and shouted, "Pick on someone your own size, ya bully!"

"Oh, oh," Briella cried.

"We have to do something," Scout murmured. "Don't panic. Don't panic."

The tabby cat said, "Mind your own business, boofhead. This does not concern you."

"I won't let you hurt the female."

"I'm not going to hurt her, idiot."

"That's right because I'm going to stop you."

The tabby cat laughed. "You and who's army?"

Stubs took a couple of steps forward. The tabby cat growled menacingly. Stubs was frightened beyond belief but refused to acknowledge his fear. He took another step forward. The tabby declined to accept Stub's challenge. He went for the female and wrapped his mouth over the back of her neck. Stubs leapt towards the tabby. Scout flew to the rear of Stub's neck and landed abruptly. Her heels dug into his skin before she managed to place herself in a sitting position. She had barely grasped his fur with both hands when he began to twist his body savagely.

Briella looked on with a mixture of shock and amusement. She didn't know whether to laugh or gasp. She conjured an image of a cowboy riding a bull and couldn't really see any difference between that and what she was currently witnessing. Briella was desperate to give Scout a hand but was afraid of releasing more fairy dust. All she could do was keep watch and be ready to offer assistance if Scout happened to fall or become injured some other way.

Stubs was terrified. Something was biting him on the neck, and no matter how hard he tried to dislodge it, the rotten thing wouldn't let go. He decided to seek another method of detachment. Stubs sat on his backside and spun his head around. He nipped at his neck and managed to grip Scout's leg between his teeth.

He tugged at her roughly. Her scream was lost beneath the noises of the felines. She let go of his fur, hoping he would do the same to her limb. He did not. Not to be deterred, Scout swung herself up and flicked her arms at his mouth. Fairy dust flew from her pores and landed on his face. He opened his mouth and coughed long and hard, spitting up a hairball in the process. Briella hovered like a parent who could see the danger approaching their child but was uncertain of which path to take that would keep them safe.

Scout flew onto Stubs' shoulders and fisted his fur gently. When he didn't make any sudden movements, she tugged slightly with her right hand and waited to see how he would respond. His ear twitched faintly, but he didn't attempt to throw her off. She kicked her legs lightly, wishing she had allowed Briella to give her a riding lesson.

Stubs flinched and looked set to protest, so Scout stilled herself and waited patiently. She hoped that he would not be distracted by the other cats that appeared ready to take their leave. Scout leant forward and rubbed his fur in smooth, circular motions. Stubs relaxed beneath her fingers, so she continued the action for quite some time.

When she felt he was suitably calmed, she tried again. A light kick of her legs had him standing on his feet and looking over his shoulder. His eyes widened slightly when he spotted her there. She grinned at him self-consciously, hoping he wouldn't realise her lack of riding skills. Scout wished she could trade places with Briella. It seemed she was going to have another opportunity to step out of her comfort zone. Scout spoke gently to him, even though she knew he wouldn't understand a word she said. She hoped that he would get the gist of her tone and comprehend that she meant him no harm. Although she was still unclear how she was going to get him to go where she wanted.

"We should have filled our pockets with cat biscuits!" Briella yelled at Scout.

Scout snorted, "Yeah, that would have helped a lot." They would have only been able to carry two each.

"We could have flown ahead and dropped them like Hansel. The kitten would have followed behind, eating them as he went."

"Who's Hansel?" Scout asked.

"You know, Hansel and Gretel."

"No, who are they?"

"Never mind. It was a great idea, but as we don't have any biscuits, I don't know how we are going to get the kitten to go anywhere tonight."

"Why does he have to go anywhere?"

"It's not safe here. We are out in the open, and the moonlight is so bright we are too visible to predators. We would be safe back in the forest among the trees."

"Like we were when the tabby came?"

Briella grimaced, "Good point. At least they are gone now, and the kitten didn't even notice."

"Yeah, we got lucky there. This little fella seems to notice everything. Have you noted how curious he is?"

"No, but that gives me an idea."

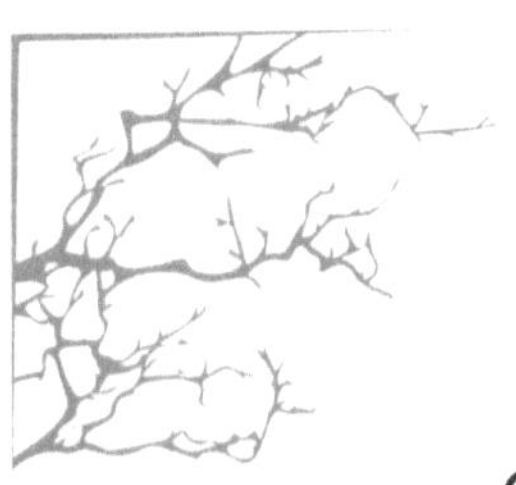

Chapter Sixteen

Briella shoved a hand into her pocket and pulled out her notebook and pencil. She quickly sketched the outline of a turtle dove and shaded it enough to make it appear 3D. She tore the page out of her book then sprinkled some fairy dust on it. The bird flew off the page, catching Stubs' attention.

The bird flapped aimlessly, unsure of its surroundings. Briella called to the bird and instructed it to follow her. She zoomed towards the forest, the bird trailing close behind. Stubs gave chase, though he still felt full from his last meal. However, the memory of the sweetness of the dove meat could not be shaken, and he figured it would be just as delicious the second time around.

They raced across the meadows, the moon supplying enough light to ensure they headed in the right direction. Scout held on for dear life. Stubs didn't seem to mind the tightness of her grip. She noticed the way his fur rippled when she tugged too harshly. His eyes never strayed from his prey and his paws never faltered in their stride. It didn't take Scout long to begin enjoying the ride. Although, after a while, she discovered her bottom was becoming quite tender.

"Are we there yet?" she muttered beneath her breath and then laughed. The quickest way to upset a parent was to ask that question. She considered screaming it at Briella but didn't want to upset her friend's feelings. Briella had come up with the perfect solution to getting Stubs to a safer place to spend the night. Scout certainly couldn't have done as good a job. There were some benefits to Briella's magic being on the fritz.

They reached the edge of the forest, and things became a little more complicated. Once they stepped inside, their light source would disappear. Thanks to Briella's great idea with the bird, it sparked another in Scout. She flew up to join her friend. "Do you think you could draw a lantern, Briella? You could make it come to life, and I could fill it with fairy dust."

"What a great idea," Briella said, clasping her hands in front of her. "I don't know why we didn't think of this before."

"I didn't know you carried a notebook and pen with you," Scout returned.

Briella rolled her eyes, but as she had turned to look at Stubs, it was lost to the darkness. Briella convinced the bird to land on a nearby branch. Stubs sized up the tree, wondering if it were possible to scale its bark. Scout encouraged Briella to draw quickly, afraid that Stubs would catch the bird, infecting him with Briella's magic.

The moment the two lanterns were created and filled with fairy dust, they moved inside the forest. Stubs had not had a chance to attempt the climb, but the idea remained in the back of his mind. He leapt over logs and skirted around bushes, though the fairies wondered how he was able to complete such feats with his eyes looking up rather than where he was going. Scout was highly impressed. Briella was rightfully terrified. "How could you live out here with these dangerous creatures?" she asked Scout.

Scout sighed. Briella had lost so many of her fairy instincts by living a comfortable life with April. Scout realised it was going to be a more significant task than she had initially thought in teaching Briella how to live as a fairy, once again.

"I am a fairy. How else am I supposed to live?" Scout answered.

"Like me. Luckily, April is building us a house. Imagine the dangers you would have to face by making this forest your permanent residence." Scout thought about her previous home in the Gold Coast Hinterlands. As far as the wildlife was concerned, the danger was no different. The human element, however, was a different story. There were far more chances of being detected by a human in this area of the country than her previous home.

'Yeah, lucky."

They arrived at the village, and Briella helped the bird settle in for the night. She found an abandoned nest for the dove to use as its temporary home. Then she returned to Scout to find that Stubs was nowhere in sight.

"Where is he?" Briella shrieked.

"In the bushes. He's going to the toilet."

"Oh!" Briella huffed. "I should probably go myself."

"Use the outhouse. It's over there," she pointed, making sure the light picked up the action.

"There is a building just for that?"

"Yes, Briella. A communal bathroom."

"How gross!" she exclaimed.

"You could always go in the bushes with Stubs," Scout suggested.

"The outhouse will be fine," Briella assured her.

Stubs returned while Briella was away. He looked around for the bird but could not find it. He raised his nose in the air, but could not detect its scent. He lay on his tummy, with his front paws spread and his nose touching the dirt. Then he closed his eyes and began to snore.

Briella came back quite concerned. "Should he sound like that?"

Scout shrugged. "I don't know. I generally stay away from cats wherever possible."

Briella watched the rise and fall of his chest. When his rhythm stayed consistent, she settled in for a chat. "Do you think April or Force will keep the cat and her kittens?"

Scout didn't have to think about it at all. "Force will definitely hang onto them if the mother cat consents to stay." She nodded in Stubs direction, "I think he will push to keep this one, either way."

"The mother cat won't allow that," Briella frowned.

"Oh, I think she will. This one is going to be heaps of trouble. He seems to be easily distracted."

Briella appeared doubtful. "He didn't take his eyes off that bird for anything."

"No," Scout agreed. "But he did take his eyes off those two cats."

"I nearly had a heart attack when he challenged that tabby."

"Me too."

"I can't believe he thought he was going to hurt her."

"He is just a kitten," Scout reminded her.

"True," Briella murmured. Stubs ears twitched as they spoke. "Should we go inside?"

"Yeah, we should let him get some sleep."

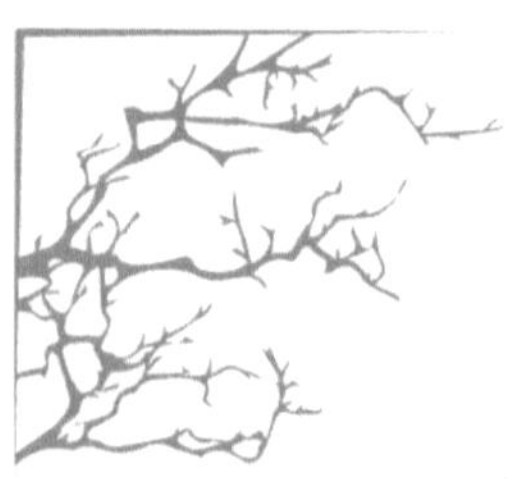

Chapter Seventeen

The first rays of the day breached the horizon chasing the shadows away. The extreme change in the skyline was lost among the trees in the forest. The fairies were taken by surprise by the gradual lightening of their surroundings.

They were laughing so hard, they missed the quiet meowing of the kitten they were supposed to be caring for. Stubs, curious as ever, peered through the window of the hut. He gave Briella such a fright, she launched to her feet. Scout pushed back from the table, afraid of a possible dust shower. Briella's expression became crestfallen when she witnessed Scout's response. Scout sported the appearance of a guilty person when she noticed how her action affected her friend.

"I'm sorry, Briella."

"Don't be," she replied, heading for the door. "I'd be afraid to be around me too if I was you."

"I just spent the entire night with you, Briella. I am not afraid to be with you. I am a little cautious of what your magic is capable of, however. Please don't hold that against me."

"I won't," she replied, but Scout was doubtful of her tone.

It sounded like she would definitely hold it against her. She had to distract Briella, and Scout knew just what to say. "I think you should sprinkle April with your fairy dust."

"What did you say?" Briella shrieked. "How could you suggest such a thing?"

"Easily," she shrugged, "We know from the kitten that your magic is not going to kill or maim her permanently. She will get a fright and worry that her life will never be the same. But then dawn will come, and she will discover that it wasn't so bad once she takes the time to think about it and she might be more open to taking a chance on a relationship with Force."

"You've got rocks in your head," Briella shook her head. "I am not doing that." She stepped outside, and her heart melted when Stubs rubbed himself against her. "You are so gorgeous," she cooed gently, wrapping her arms around his neck. She stopped abruptly when she realised how dangerously she was behaving. "Oops, nearly did it again."

Scout was stunned by Briella's reaction. She had been terrified by the kittens at the pub, not wanting to be in the same room as them and then lying to April about her feelings. Now she acted as though she was meeting an old friend that she had longed to catch-up with. Scout observed the gentle way Briella approached the kitty, and the tender strokes she applied to his cheeks. The kitten meowed loudly. "He must be hungry," she said. "Wait with him while I go get Force."

"Okay," Scout yelled after Briella, who had already begun the journey to the pub. She eyed the kitten cautiously. "How did you manage to get separated from your family? I can't wait to hear your story. You need to stay here for a minute while I take care of something. Don't go anywhere," she waggled her finger at his face.

Stubs stared at her with curious eyes. He watched her fly away before he realised he had missed an opportunity to practise his technique. His instincts to hunt weren't as strong in his kitten body. He scrutinised his surroundings for something interesting to do. His ears pricked forward as a rustling sound came from his left. He stretched out his body and listened intently. Another crunching of leaves had him crouch-walking in that direction. By the time Scout reappeared he had miraculously disappeared.

"Oh dear," she exclaimed, hovering a couple of metres off the ground to get a better view. She spun in a circle but was unable to see him anywhere. She cupped her hands around her mouth and called to him. Though she listened carefully, she was unable to detect a response. Scout flew to the nearest branch and sent out an energy burst. Searching for an indigenous creature of Earth didn't reap a reply. "Briella is going to kill me," she spluttered, choosing the direction of the creek to begin her search, and hoping for the best.

It took her a few minutes to locate him, which wasn't bad considering she was in the forest. She watched him with quiet amusement. He was following a blue tongue lizard twice his size. What he planned to do with it when he caught it was anyone's guess. The lizard would more than likely bite him before Stubs had a chance to work out how to wrap his little mouth around the reptile's body.

A field mouse raced through some leaves to his left. Stubs jumped slightly, his claws popping out of four paws. He spun his body around and chased after the rodent.

"Wait!" Scout yelled, wondering how long it would be before Briella returned. She kept him in her sights until he ran out of puff and squatted on the ground defeated. His little head rested on his front legs, and he closed his eyes. Scout wanted to tell him what a great job he had done tracking but knew he wouldn't understand a word she said. Instead, she merely kept an eye on him to make sure he was safe while she waited for the others to arrive.

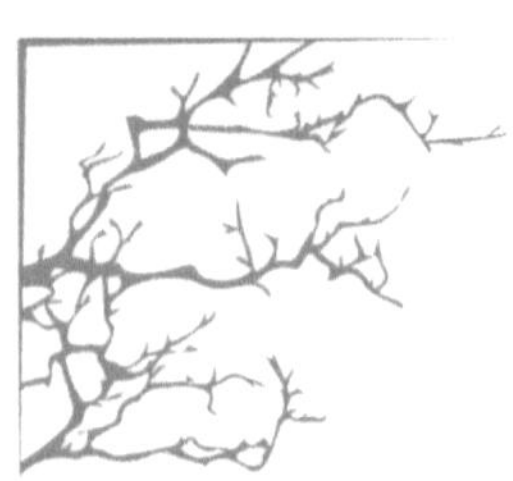

Chapter Eighteen

Force and Briella arrived soon enough. Briella flew down to Stubs' level and checked him over carefully. He raised his head with a semblance of interest that didn't last long. He lowered his head, still exhausted after his latest burst of energy.

Briella turned to Scout, "What is wrong with him?"

"He's been chasing our local wildlife. He is just tired."

"He must be hungry," she surmised.

"I doubt it. Not after the feast he devoured last night."

Briella didn't look convinced. "Let's get him home to his mother so she can feed him."

Force picked the kitten up and studied him closely. "You look just like the kitten at the pub.

How did I miss you?"

Scout flew nearer to Force, "Judging by his earlier behaviour, I would say he was off exploring something when you counted them."

"But I was talking to him at the time," Force replied.

"Then perhaps his sibling looks the same as him and was off somewhere else."

Force nodded, "That is plausible. Come on, little guy, let's get you home."

The fairies used Force's shoulder as a means of transport home. Force took his time walking through the trees then over the open fields. He breathed in the fresh air and took joy in being outdoors. Children's laughter that would not have been heard with natural human hearing brought a wistful smile to his lips. His thoughts turned to April, and for the first time in three thousand years, he wished that he could father a child of his own.

Force waited for the fairies to flutter away before sneaking the kitten in through the backdoor and heading quickly up the stairs. He managed to beat them to the room. They found the window of their usual entry and exit was closed but they couldn't have entered anyway because their way inside was blocked by the mother cat who continued her appraisal of the surroundings through the window. Force entered the room, and the cat jumped from the windowsill. She padded over to him and meowed long and loud. He knelt down beside her, holding the kitten out in his hand. "Is this what you've been looking for?"

She pressed her nose to Stubs' and purred contentedly. She meowed gently and began washing his face with her tongue. Force placed him gently on the floor and opened the window. "Sorry," he told the fairies. "I forgot we closed the window. April was afraid the mother would jump out and hurt herself."

"Do you think she was looking for him?" Briella asked.

"No doubt," Force replied, brimming with happiness. "I'm glad you found him. I'd hate to think what might have happened to him if you hadn't. Just imagine if he'd come across a tom cat or a fox or some other predator. I shudder to think."

"Me too," Scout smiled. "Imagine if we hadn't been brought here by the Jealousy Monsters. His mother would have died, and all of these kittens would have followed her."

Briella said, "You don't suppose Destiny . . ."

They looked at one another then laughed. Linking elbows, Scout said, "Up for some breakfast?"

"Sure," Briella stated with a stomach growl for emphasis. They flew to the cupboard to retrieve their mushrooms.

Titles by Marnie Atwell

Starlight Investigations

Jealousy Monsters

Vampire

Phantasm

Halloween Madness

The Pumpkin Patch

The House of Horrors

The Spirited Scarecrow

The Curious Kitten

About the Author

Marnie is an Australian author who lives in South-East Queensland with her husband and two children. When she is not dreaming up new adventures for her characters, Marnie enjoys creating pictures in Daz 3D; playing the piano; reading paranormal romance novels; and spending time with family and friends. Not necessarily in that order.

Visit her website at: www.marnieatwell.com for more books, contact details, and free downloads.

The next book in this series is:

The Sneaky Skeleton